For Sue, with love   AMcA

For my parents   AM

Text copyright © 1992 by Angela McAllister
Illustrations copyright © 1992 by Anne Magill
All rights reserved. No part of this book may be reproduced or transmitted in any form or
by any means, electronic or mechanical, including photocopying, recording, or by any
information storage and retrieval system, without permission in writing from the
Publisher. Macmillan Publishing Company is part of the Maxwell Communication Group
of Companies. Macmillan Publishing Company, 866 Third Avenue, New York, NY 10022.

First published by All Books for Children, a division of the All Children's Company Ltd.,
London, England.

First American edition
Printed in Hong Kong
1   3   5   7   9   10   8   6   4   2
Library of Congress Cataloging-in-Publication Data is available.
ISBN 0-02-765366-8

Jessie's Journey

Written by Angela McAllister
Illustrated by Anne Magill

Macmillan Publishing Company   New York
Maxwell Macmillan International   New York   Oxford   Singapore   Sydney

Jessie was going away.
   First she heard about her journey . . .
about tickets and trains and
"nothing like the old days."

Then she was
told about her
journey . . .

about getting up
before the sun and
a taxi ride to
the station.

Then she wondered about her journey. . . .

Maybe there would be mountains,
like Rosa's trip to see her brother.

Maybe there would be a parade,
like Ed's visit to his aunt.

Maybe there would be midnight, like
when Anna went to stay with her dad.

Then Jessie dreamed her journey . . .
and she was racing through the night on a train of
crazy dreams. The engine spat fireworks that lit up
the sky. Snow monsters waved as the cars raced past
and the conductor turned into a juggling carnival clown.

Then it was time to go
on Jessie's journey. . . .
The station had a roof as high as
the sky. The conductor's whistle
screeched like a parakeet and
the great engines
hummed.

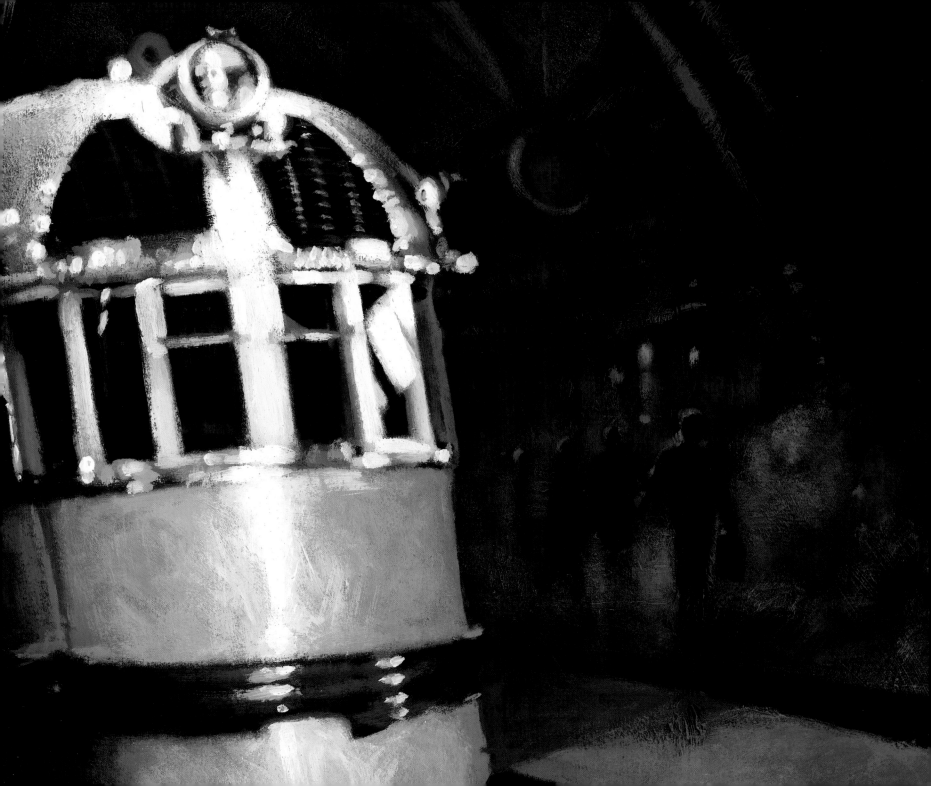

Jessie found her seat as the train
started to creep into the cool gray
light of morning.

Out of the city and into the town, snaking through hills and speeding through vales, chimneys and spires, sheep and cows, apples and pears and galleon clouds, Jessie's journey rolled on and on.

And Grandpa was waiting with pockets full
of peppermints and the beach for his backyard.

Soon Jessie slipped into
bed and dreamed of all the
journeys yet to come. . . .